Julia's House Goes Home

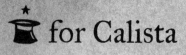

for Calista

:01
First Second

Published by First Second
First Second is an imprint
of Roaring Brook Press,
a division of Holtzbrinck Publishing
Holdings Limited Partnership
120 Broadway, New York, NY 10271
firstsecondbooks.com
mackids.com

Library of Congress Cataloging-in-Publication
Data is available.

Our books may be purchased in bulk for promotional,
educational, or business use. Please contact your local
bookseller or the Macmillan Corporate and Premium Sales
Department at (800) 221-7945 ext. 5442 or by
email at MacmillanSpecialMarkets@macmillan.com.

FIRST
EDITION

First edition, 2021
Edited by Calista Brill and Kiara Valdez
Jacket design by Ben Hatke and Kirk Benshoff
Interior book design by Kirk Benshoff

BY ART
WE LIVE

Printed in China by RR Donnelley Asia Printing Solutions Ltd.,
Dongguan City, Guangdong Province

ISBN 978-1-250-76932-9
10 9 8 7 6 5 4 3 2 1

Don't miss your next favorite book from First Second! For the latest
updates go to firstsecondnewsletter.com and sign up for our enewsletter.

Julia's House Goes Home

Ben Hatke

:01
First Second
New York

Julia's house roamed the
high hills, looking for a home.

And so, when Julia saw the Perfect Spot glittering in the distance, she told her creatures, "That's where we're going."

And the creatures all cheered.

But the path from the
high hills to the valley
was ROCKY and
ROUGH.

"BE CAREFUL!"
shouted Julia.

But it was TOO LATE.

Julia's house rolled away—

WITHOUT JULIA!

DOWN,

DOWN,

DOWN

she fell.

When Julia sat up, she was in a Deep Dark Place.

She had nothing left but the sign from her front door.

But there was a tunnel ahead, so she followed that.

Just as Julia was getting really lonely,

a familiar face appeared in the dark.

It was Patched Up Kitty!

"Come on," said Julia.

"Let's go find our house."

The cave opened out
onto a shadowy wood.

The house had surely
come this way.

Goblins and folletti
were scattered about.

"Follow me!" called Julia.

"We're off to find our house!"

They walked on until a sweet
voice cut through the gloom.

It was a unicorn.

"I found your mermaid," it said.

The mermaid asked if the unicorn could come along.

Julia looked at her sign—the one that meant *welcome to all lost creatures*.

"We'll make room," she said.

The path of the house led
through the gates of a graveyard.

The ghost was there, having drifted from the house as it rolled, with a host of specters and shades.

"We'll make room!" said Julia.

"Just follow me!"

On and on they marched, and
everywhere it was the same.

Old friends found.

New faces joining in.

There were more lost creatures in the
world than Julia had ever imagined.

They all saw her sign and followed.

"We'll make room!" she told them all.

But she began to wonder...

When they stopped to rest, the creatures talked
about tea and toast and warm beds for everyone.

Julia sat apart.

Wondering turned to worry.

"There won't be enough room,"
she said to herself.

But still she led them on.

Until—

Julia looked down at the battered knob from her front door.

And she knew she had to tell them.

"ATTENTION, PLEASE!" Julia called.

The creatures all looked up at her, with their teeth and talons and horns.

Julia took a deep breath.

"I have something to say," she began. "It's about the house—"

But before she could continue,

the ground began to SHAKE.

"DID SOMEONE SAY *HOUSE*?"
a voice rumbled.

It was a mountain king, the largest of all trolls.

"A HOUSE ROLLED 'CROSS MY HEAD AND JUST O'ER THAT HILL," it said.

"WASN'T MUCH LEFT OF IT, THOUGH."

"HOORAY!" the creatures cheered. "WE'RE ALMOST THERE! KEEP GOING!"

Julia gathered up her sign and climbed the last hill.

And there it was.
The Perfect Spot.

It was the very spot she'd
seen glimmering in the
distance.

Except...

It wasn't perfect.

What Julia had seen was nothing but the sun glinting off the scraps in a junkyard.

And there was nothing left of Julia's house

but the front door.

Julia put the doorknob back on her door.

And she put down her sign.
The one that meant *all are welcome*.

She turned to the creatures who had followed her on the long march across the countryside.

"I'm sorry," she said.

"I let you down."

"LET US DOWN?!?" they said.
"NEVER!"

"WE HAVE EVERYTHING
WE NEED!"

The creatures set to work.

They worked for a
long, long time.

And together...

They made a new home.

With room for everyone.

They called it Julia's Town.

The end.